THE BATMAN

Maximum Justice

By Devan Aptekar

Based on the teleplays "Call of the Cobblepot" by Steven Melching
and "Traction" by Adam Beechen

BATMAN created by Bob Kane

SCHOLASTIC INC.

New York   Toronto   London   Auckland   Sydney
Mexico City   New Delhi   Hong Kong   Buenos Aires

ISBN 0-439-72778-2

Book design by Bethany Dixon
© 2005 DC Comics.

12 11 10 9 8 7 6 5 4 3 2 1   5 6 7 8 9 10/0

Printed in the U.S.A.
First printing, March 2005

Before there was a Boy Wonder, or even a Commissioner Gordon, there was Batman.

Batman will stop at nothing to protect Gotham City from danger. His secret identity: young billionaire Bruce Wayne, the honorary head of Wayne Enterprises. Hunted by the police as well as bizarre villains bent on his destruction, Batman carries on with his war on crime, helped only by his longtime butler, Alfred.

The nights in Gotham City are long. And deadly. But criminals beware — Batman stalks the night in Gotham now, and he's here to stay.

PART ONE

CALL OF THE COBBLEPOT

Gotham City's towering buildings rose into the leaden-gray night. High above the skyline, the edge of the moon peeked out from behind a long, low cloud. Suddenly, the night's quiet was broken by a horrified scream.

"My necklace! It's gone!"

The screaming came from a balcony window in one of Gotham City's fanciest apartment buildings.

"My jeweled necklace!"

The clouds continued to gather around the tops of the tall stone buildings, covering the moon completely. With a faint swooshing sound, an owl sped through the air and disappeared into the darkness.

Anyone who knew about birds would have been very surprised to see that owl. Owls like that did not usually live in Gotham. However, nobody spotted the strange owl . . . or the small bundle glittering in its talons.

Fifteen minutes later, police cars pulled up

at the building. The detective team of Ethan Bennett and Ellen Yin rode the elevator up to the penthouse to investigate.

"Third high-rise this week, all just the same," said Detective Bennett as he and his partner inspected the crime scene. "No fingerprints, no forced entry, no physical evidence of any kind."

Detective Yin stood next to him. She shook her head wearily. "I'd say it sounds like our Batman, *if* he were a burglar," she replied.

They went back into the living room, stretching a long band of yellow Do Not Enter tape across the closed door.

From the darkness outside the balcony window, a pair of eyes watched them leave.

Batman gathered his cape around himself and eased the balcony window open, stepping into the now-empty room. He quickly went to work. He clipped a pair of high-tech goggles on over his mask. The lenses glowed red, showing him a thermal image of the room.

Through the goggles, Batman could see the two detectives' footprints ending at the closed door. The prints were fading away as they cooled. A few seconds later, they had disappeared. Nothing else seemed out of the ordinary.

Batman pressed a button on his goggles and the lenses turned blue. He grabbed a small flashlight from his Utility Belt and switched it on. The beam was invisible to the naked eye, but through his special goggles, Batman could see the room bathed in ultraviolet light.

He moved to the dresser, seeing something that the detectives had missed: faint claw scratches in the wood. Batman pressed a button on his Utility Belt and snapped a digital photo of the four jagged lines.

He ran the UV flashlight across the floor. *Now what's that?* thought Batman, as his gaze fixed on one area of the floor. He pulled out a small pair of forceps and a little container. He snagged the tiny piece of fluff he had spotted and dropped it carefully into the clear vial.

He folded up his goggles and slid them into a slot on his belt, and then peered at what he'd found — a fragment of a feather. Before he could check out the feather more closely, the doorknob rattled and turned.

The two detectives entered, ducking under the police tape.

"I thought I put it on the . . ." Detective Bennett's words trailed off. His mouth gaped in astonishment as the sliver of light from the bright living room fell across a dark, but instantly recognizable figure.

Detective Yin pointed fiercely. "Batman!"

3

A breeze blew through the long curtains, swirling them into the room like two ghosts. Batman was already outside.

By the time Detective Yin had scrambled out to the balcony, Batman was soaring through the air away from them.

"Freeze!" shouted Detective Yin.

Ignoring her, Batman rode down his zip-line, picking up speed as he slid. It was dizzying, zipping down toward the sidewalk pavement across the street. Holding tight to the Bat-grapnel with one hand, Batman activated his Bat-wave Transmitter. Two blocks away, in a narrow alley, the Batcycle roared to life.

Batman jumped off near the end of the zip-line, using his cape as a parachute to slow his fall. He landed hard in a crouch and immediately sprang to his feet and leaped onto the Batcycle as it zoomed up to meet him.

To escape the area, Batman had to avoid several police officers, but it wasn't that difficult. Not when he had so many secret entrances to the Batcave to use. The detective team of Bennett and Yin rushed out into the street, but Batman was nowhere to be found.

Detective Bennett could not help being impressed. Even though he knew Detective Yin didn't trust the Caped Crusader, Bennett had begun to respect him.

"Go, Bats," he murmured encouragingly into the night.

Bruce Wayne peered intently into a high-tech microscope. He still had most of his costume on, but he had removed his cape and the bulletproof, rubberized mask that slipped over his head.

"Hey, Alfred, check this out." Bruce hadn't even glanced up from the microscope, yet he had heard Alfred approaching. Most people could not have heard Alfred's nearly silent footsteps, but Bruce Wayne was not most people.

Alfred carefully hung up the expensive, tasteful change of clothes he'd been carrying and walked over to Bruce. Alfred was the only person in all of Gotham — in the whole world, in fact — who knew Batman's secret identity.

Bruce hit a switch as Alfred approached and the microscope's view was displayed on a large view-panel hanging in front of them. The tiny fragment of a feather from the apartment was magnified a hundred times in crisp detail.

"*Strix nebulosa lapponica*," murmured Bruce. He tapped a few buttons on one of the computers, and a photo of a great gray owl appeared next to the feather. "A subspecies of owl, native to northern Eurasia. But what's it doing in Gotham?"

Alfred didn't answer. He knew that at times like this, Bruce was just thinking aloud. He watched as Bruce tapped a button on his Utility Belt, sending a digital photo up onto the monitor.

"These scratches from the victim's dressing table match the owl's talon span. Alfred, someone has trained a bird to perform burglaries."

Alfred cleared his throat. "Without suggesting that I'm not sufficiently impressed with your deductive powers, Master Bruce, I must remind you that you have a gala fund-raiser to host."

Bruce frowned at him. "Right, Alfred. Tomorrow night."

"Sir," said Alfred, "it *is* tomorrow night."

Bruce shrugged and leaned back toward the microscope, trying to ignore the thought of partygoers arriving upstairs in the Wayne Mansion loft.

Alfred continued, "We wouldn't want any guests growing suspicious of how 'billionaire bachelor' Bruce Wayne really spends his time after dark, would we?"

Bruce sighed and stood up. "Okay. I'll put in an appearance." He began to walk out of the Batcave.

Alfred picked up the hanger of clothes he had brought into the Batcave and wiggled them meaningfully. "Might I suggest more *appropriate* evening attire?" he called after Bruce.

The party was the event of the year . . . or at least of the month. Outside the mansion, photographers were lined up behind a velvet rope, trying to snap pictures of the arriving guests.

There was a lot of noise, but one sound sliced through the others — a strange laugh. Not quite a duck's quack . . . not quite a donkey's braying . . . it was a *nyuk, nyuk* one minute and a *mrah, mrah, mrah* the next. The crowd parted for a group of three people walking confidently past the limousines. They stopped in front of the photographers.

"Make way! The Oz-meister is in the *hizzouse!*" yelled the short, pear-shaped man in the middle. He laughed again with a weird honking sound. Standing at either side of him were two tall women, one in a long green robe, one in a long blue robe. They both wore blank-faced white masks and only their eyes could be seen through them.

The odd, short man was wearing a nice tuxedo

that looked like it was from the style of over one hundred years ago. He had a long curved nose, a monocle screwed in tight over one eye, a tall black top hat, and white gloves that made his hands look like flippers. In one of his flipperlike hands, he held a long black umbrella that he occasionally twirled around.

The weird trio pushed their way forward and entered the party. Inside, music filled the air — whatever space was left between the people. A fantastic light show played across the room — blues, oranges, reds, purples — all changing with the beats of the songs being spun by a DJ. The trio didn't pause to dance or chat with other guests, but instead made straight for the host of the party.

The short pear-shaped man in the tux shoved Alfred aside and yelled, "Bruce Wayne! King of the castle! Ruler of the roost!"

Bruce was taken aback by this stranger, but shook the gloved flipper-like hand that was thrust toward him. "Have we met?" he asked.

"Cobblepot! Oswald Cobblepot of the Newport Cobblepots."

Alfred was visibly startled for a moment, but

then quickly composed himself.

Oswald leaned in toward Bruce. "Call me Ozzy," he honked. "You know, we've got a lot in common, you and I — we're young, rich . . . *handsome.*"

"I'm not sure I've heard of — " Bruce began.

"I've been abroad for a while," Oswald interrupted. "Just got back from a tour of Northern Europe and Asia. Met these friends of mine there." He pointed at the two silent women with the blank-faced masks. They turned to stare at Bruce, but didn't speak or even nod their heads.

"Nice to meet you all," said Bruce. He was feeling a little wary of these people, but he was hosting a party and knew that he must be kind to his guests. "Please excuse me," Bruce said and moved on to mingle with his other guests.

A few steps away, he turned back to share a meaningful glance with Alfred. Alfred clearly knew something about this man, but what? He'd have to find out later. Bruce rubbed his left eyebrow before walking off, a signal for Alfred to keep an eye on these three. Alfred straightened up. He had no intention of letting them get out of his sight.

Oswald turned, reached over, and pulled the silver serving tray right out of Alfred's hands. He quickly pushed the appetizers on the tray into a line. Then he tilted the tray down toward his face and all the snacks slid into his mouth.

Alfred was appalled.

Ozzy laughed that strange, almost-quacking laugh through a mouthful of food. "More shrimp puffs and be quick about it!" he yelled. "And no skimping on the mayo this time!"

Alfred felt closer to losing his temper than he ever had before. He gritted his teeth and pulled a sheet of paper from the inside pocket of his serving jacket. "I will have you know — " he began, but just then Bruce returned.

"Everything okay here, Alfred?" Bruce asked.

"I was about to inform Mr. Cobblepot that his name does *not* appear on the guest list." Alfred tried to calm his voice down so he wouldn't cause a scene.

"Let me see that," said Ozzy. He grabbed the list from Alfred, dropping the serving tray to the floor. Ozzy scanned the list, shaking his head with disgust. His two companions read over his shoulder, their eyes moving behind their blank white masks.

"Hmph," said Ozzy. "An oversight. Best teach your help some manners, Brucie." With that, the trio pushed away toward the exit.

6

Bruce immediately started after them, but then turned back to Alfred for some quick answers. He wanted to know what he was getting himself into, especially because he was not dressed as Batman. "Cobblepot?"

Alfred almost shook with anger. "Exactly, sir. My grandfather used to butler for them back in England, and they were an obnoxious lot then, as well. Grandfather worked himself to the bone for those snobs and they treated him hideously. Then they had the nerve to fire him!"

Bruce nodded thoughtfully. He placed one hand on Alfred's shoulder for a moment. "Keep an eye on the party for me. I'll be right back."

Outside, there was no sign of the trio amongst the chaos of photographers, cars, chauffeurs, and people coming and going. Bruce looked around for anything out of the ordinary, while trying his best not to be noticed. After all, he was Bruce Wayne, young billionaire and host of the charity mega-party.

Then he caught sight of something — a mysterious, unmarked car parked just outside the gates of Wayne Manor. Bruce jogged up to the car and knocked on the driver's window. "You know, trespassing is against the law," he said calmly.

The window rolled down. Detective Ethan Bennett, an old friend of Bruce's from childhood, sat behind the wheel. "Oops," Detective Bennett said. "Busted."

Bruce smiled, happy to see him. He bent down to see who was in the passenger seat. It was an Asian-American woman with long black hair and a no-nonsense expression on her face.

"I see you've brought a guest, Ethan."

"My partner," said Detective Bennett.

"I'm Bruce," he introduced himself with a smile.

The woman looked at him for a moment before responding, "Detective Yin."

Of course, thought Bruce. *They were together investigating the apartment robbery.* He composed his thoughts and went back into host mode. "Why don't you both come join the party?"

"Not tonight," Bennett replied. "We're on the clock." Then he cleared his throat and switched over to a more professional tone of voice. "Chief's orders: Keep an eye on high-profile events, with that string of robberies and all."

"Okay. Another time, then. I appreciate the protection." Bruce smiled again. "I'd better get back, Ethan. Nice meeting you, Detective Yin."

Bruce hurried back to the mansion and did his best to be patient for another few hours until the party was over, the guests were gone, and the major cleaning was finished.

"It's odd, sir," said Alfred, when they were finally alone. "I was certain I'd heard the Cobblepot fortune had been squandered. They had to leave England to avoid the shame."

"The shame would be if you didn't get some sleep, Alfred. It's been a long night. And try not to dream of these Cobblepots."

"And you, sir?"

"That robber owl is still on my mind." Bruce walked toward a paneled wall and tapped his fingers against it in a quick and complicated sequence. One of the panels unlocked with a *whoosh* and swung inward into darkness. "Batman has some birdwatching to do," continued Bruce before jumping into the dark space. The panel swung shut behind him and sealed itself so that the outline of the door was completely invisible.

Alfred stood for a moment, lost in thought. Then his eyes bugged out a little as he remembered something — the silver serving tray! He ran to where it had last been but it was gone. In fact, he hadn't seen it since Oswald and his companions left. He remembered seeing a glint of silver as they'd walked off, but Alfred had been too angry and shocked at the time to realize what it was.

"He stole it, just to spite me!" Alfred frowned . . . but then had an idea. "Well, Grandfather Pennyworth would have wanted to know what became of the Cobblepots, after all. . . ."

7

Batman perched on a stone gargoyle that jutted out near the top of a building. The gargoyle was curled around itself, and one of its large shoulders gave Batman all the space he needed to balance high above the city.

The view was amazing. Gotham stretched on and on into the cloud-filled, moonless night. Batman kept almost perfectly still, watching the sky and the skyline, only his head turning slowly from side to side every so often.

Suddenly, he snapped to attention. A small point of light glimmered in the sky nearby. Then there was another one. And another one. And another!

The points of light were moving, getting closer. Batman pulled off his goggles as the specks grew until the sky around him was swarming — with birds! Owls, ravens, and vultures flapped past him in a huge flock. Each one of them held a glittering piece of jewelry in its talons or its beak.

Batman scrambled up the last few feet of the building onto the roof. He sprinted across the gravel-covered rooftop, following the flock.

The birds were getting farther away, and Batman was rapidly running out of rooftop. Three more steps left . . . two more . . . one! Batman leaped off the building into the air, pressing a button on his Utility Belt. With a loud snap, Bat-glider wings spread out from under his cape and lifted him up into the air currents.

But the birds had vanished.

Batman rose higher, searching for any sign of the flock. He spotted an owl that must have momentarily lost the others and soared toward it, pulling his glider wings tight to fit between two close buildings. Batman chased the owl through the twisting canyons of the Gotham cityscape.

The owl screeched and dove toward a deserted alley. Batman curled around the corner, as the owl dropped its treasure into a huge duffel bag that was propped open beside a car. From his position high above the alley, Batman saw that the bag was stuffed with jewels and gold. A figure moved in the shadows behind the car — a tall figure in a long green robe with a blank-faced white mask covering her face!

Whoa! thought Batman. *But where's creepy-mask number two?* He sensed something behind him and spun around — too late. A flash of blue flew at him from a fire escape.

In a blur of motion, the woman launched a kick at Batman, connecting solidly. He slammed against the opposite wall, snapping one of his glider wings in half. She landed neatly on a window ledge, but Batman spiraled out of control toward the ground!

Spinning toward the pavement, Batman had only one choice. He quickly pulled his arms free of the Bat-glider and let it fall beside him, preparing his body for a proper landing. Batman rolled with the impact of hitting the ground, narrowly avoiding the crash of the glider wings, and hopped up to his feet. He was a bit shaken, but otherwise fine.

The two white-masked women finished putting the huge, jewelry-filled duffel bag into the car and turned to face Batman. For a moment, they stood frozen in strong defensive martial arts poses, but then they launched into action. With cartwheels and handsprings, they almost seemed to fly across the alley at Batman.

Batman twisted out of the way from one powerful flip-kick in blue, but couldn't avoid the green one that came right after. He slammed backward against the brick wall behind him, knocking over a trash can.

The two women cartwheeled away and

repositioned themselves gracefully for another attack. Batman staggered to his feet, rubbing his sore jaw. "Double trouble," he muttered.

Again and again, the women flashed around Batman, kicks and punches raining down on him. He managed to avoid a lot of the attacks, but he was still getting bruised by the ones that landed. Also, the women were too nimble for him — he kept missing them.

His feet were knocked out from under him and he hopped up just in time to see that the two women had locked arms and were spinning toward him. *Uh-oh,* Batman thought before he was pummeled by a blur. He smashed into a Dumpster, denting it with the impact.

The air was knocked out of Batman's chest. He pushed himself up to his hands and knees, trying to catch his breath. He looked up so he could ready himself for the next attack, but the women had already slipped through the open windows of the car doors. The car peeled out of the alley, leaving only a cloud of dust hovering behind it.

Alfred looked up at the gate arching above his head, the word OBBLEPOT twined into the ironwork. The metal C lay on the ground near his feet. There were no signs of life.

"Well, you came *this* far, Pennyworth," Alfred whispered as he quietly walked up the overgrown driveway. Weeds and bushes on the lawn had spread unchecked, and the trees looked like misshapen monsters in the night's shadows.

Alfred peeked into a small, dirty window set in one of the large front doors. It was too dirty to see through. He sighed and took out a handkerchief to clean the glass. As soon as he touched the door, it creaked open halfway.

Alfred cautiously poked his head inside. "Hello?" he asked.

No one answered.

The inside of the Cobblepot mansion had been beautiful, but now it was shockingly filthy and falling apart. Moonlight streamed through a cracked skylight. There were cobwebs everywhere and the wallpaper was peeling. A grand staircase curved down into the foyer.

Alfred closed the door behind him, both grossed out and fascinated by the decay. "So this is what became of the Cobblepot fortune," he murmured.

Alfred glanced around and then slowly walked up the stairs, his butler-quiet footsteps echoing softly through the deserted hall.

When he reached the top, he paused to look around. Realizing that he was touching the banister, he yanked his hand away and looked at his now dust-coated glove with disgust.

"Revolting." Alfred sneezed. Creeping down the hall, he saw something gleaming on a table — his serving tray!

"Aha," Alfred whispered. Then he stiffened as he heard a loud crash downstairs — the front door being kicked open.

Ozzy strutted in, carrying a pizza box. His long black umbrella was hooked over his arm. "I'm home, my birdies!" yelled Ozzy.

Alfred crouched against the wall in the upstairs hall, clutching the silver serving tray to his chest. "Blast," he whispered.

The Batcave was dark. The only light came from the huge computer screens that hung from such thin, superstrong wire that it seemed as if they were floating. Batman tapped at a keyboard. Scanned images of newspaper articles, one after another, appeared on the screens. Most of the articles were not in English, but they all referred to mysterious burglaries and most of them had photos of luxury skyscrapers.

Batman pulled off his mask and sat down. His face was illuminated by the glow of the screens.

"Dozens of similar crimes all across Northern Europe and Asia," Bruce muttered. "Which stop last week . . . and start back up again in Gotham." He shook his head, remembering that Oswald Cobblepot had said he'd just gotten back from a tour of Northern Europe and Asia. And that owl feather he had found — the computer had said it was native to northern Eurasia.

With a start, Bruce realized where all the

Birds are stealing jewelry from Gotham high society!

Oswald Cobblepot and his masked henchwomen crash Bruce Wayne's fund-raiser.

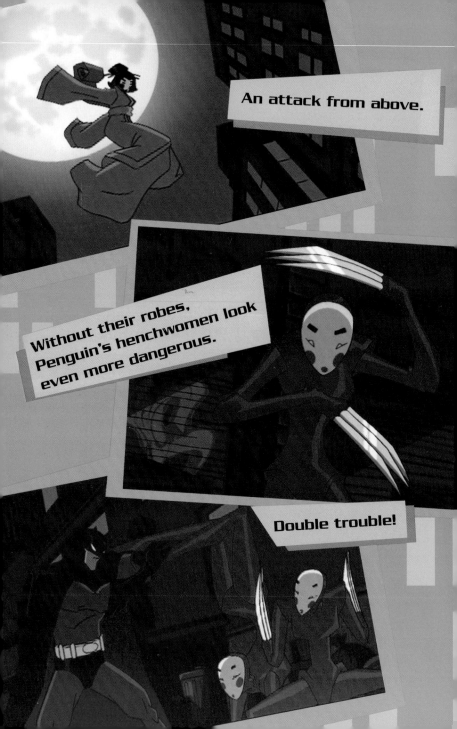

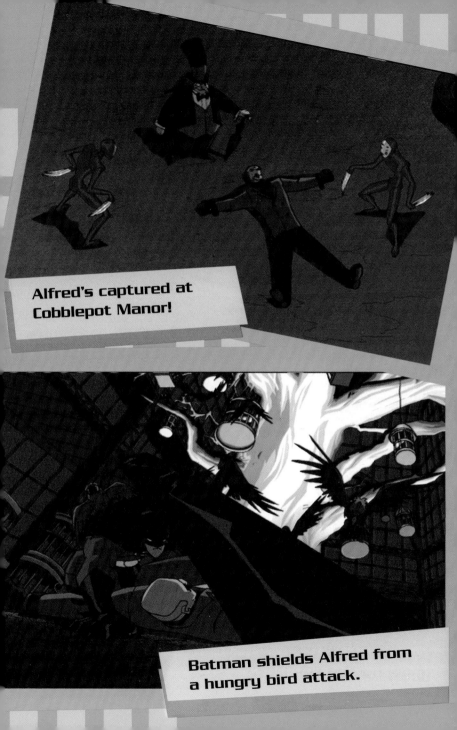

Alfred's captured at
Cobblepot Manor!

Batman shields Alfred from
a hungry bird attack.

"Bird vs. Bat!"

"This Penguin's got claws!"

Pow! Penguin goes down for the count!

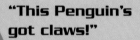

Bruce accidentally smacks Alfred with a newly invented robotic arm.

Bane tears a hole in an armored van.

Bane grows big!

"Lights out, Batman!" growls Bane.

Even in the Bat-bot, is Batman no match for Bane?

A shock to the system!

jewelry came from to fill that duffel bag. All of the richest people in Gotham had been invited to his charity fund-raiser.

Cobblepot is behind this crime spree, thought Bruce. *He used my guest list as a checklist!*

Bruce pushed an intercom button to summon Alfred. "You're going to love this," he said into the speaker.

He began typing again, bringing up a Gotham City property records database and searching for Cobblepot. "Time for me to crash *your* party, Ozzy," he said.

Bruce turned back to the intercom. "Alfred?" There was no reply. "Hmm. It's a little late to be running errands."

He reached for a nearby telephone and pressed the speed-dial button for Alfred's cell phone.

Alfred crept down the hallway toward the stairs with his serving tray. A floorboard under his foot creaked loudly and he froze.

Downstairs, Ozzy sat at a long dining table. He was lifting a slice of pizza to his mouth. It smelled delicious — Gotham City had amazing pizza. He was about to take a bite when he heard the creak.

Ozzy put down the slice and listened. But all was silent. Old mansions made noises sometimes, and anyway, he was hungry. He picked up the pizza again.

Upstairs, sweat was beading on Alfred's forehead as he waited to hear if Ozzy would respond. After a few moments, he gave a sigh of relief and took another step forward, this time being careful to avoid the creaky board.

RING! RING! His cell phone echoed through the mansion. Alfred fumbled in his pocket and turned it off, but it was too late.

"Who dares trespass in Cobblepot Manor?"

Ozzy shouted. He listened for a second before tossing his pizza aside and grabbing his umbrella. "Hide-and-seek, then!"

Oswald pulled at his umbrella handle, drawing out a long, sharp sword. The blade gleamed in the moonlight. Ozzy stalked through the mansion, murder in his eyes. He made strange gnashing and honking noises as he shuffled deeper into his home.

Alfred tiptoed away from the grand staircase, determined to find another way out. He crept down a narrow back staircase, pushing his way through cobwebs, and soon found himself in an amazingly tall, dark room. It was hard to make out anything in the gloom, except for the large windows high on the vaulted ceiling.

Alfred felt a little spooked by strange flapping noises above. He looked up and saw hundreds of pairs of gleaming eyes. Alfred stepped back, startled.

The eyes stared at him for a moment before a sharp birdcall pierced the silence. Other unseen creatures immediately took up the cry.

The calls got louder until they were almost deafening. Alfred stumbled through the darkness toward a door.

The door opened. Ozzy stood in the entranceway, holding a large candelabra that cast an eerie light into the room. "Well, well, well," said Ozzy with a laugh. "Come to help with the dusting?"

12

Alfred glanced up. The room was almost three stories high and full of birds and birdcages of all shapes and sizes. A massive, twisted, leafless tree grew in the center of the room, rising almost to the ceiling. Many of the cages hung from the tree.

Alfred dusted himself off and put on a brave front. "Actually, I just popped in to claim some missing property." He held up his serving tray.

"Fine." Ozzy sheathed his sword and grinned. "You can use it to serve me more of those shrimp puffs!"

Alfred bristled at the idea. "The days of Pennyworths serving Cobblepots are long since over," he said coldly.

"You're a Pennyworth?" Ozzy gave him a sinister smile before glancing back at the door. The two white-masked women had just come in, carrying the massive duffel bag.

Ozzy smirked. "The good old days, when Cobblepots were king, are coming back, because

I'm going to bring back our old wealth and glory."

"If you intend to do so by pilfering," said Alfred, "it may take a while."

Ozzy glared at him. "Not as long as you think, old man." He reached down and unzipped the huge duffel, pulling out two large fistfuls of jewels. The birds began squawking again in their cages.

Alfred realized that Ozzy had taken the Cobblepots to new depths — truly criminal behavior. He began backing toward the door. "Allow me to . . . fetch those shrimp puffs, right away!" said Alfred. Then he turned and made a run for it.

With a penguinlike laugh, Ozzy gestured with his umbrella. The two women grabbed Alfred, almost knocking him down. The serving tray clattered to the floor.

Ozzy walked toward the butler, tapping his umbrella. The masked women tied Alfred to hooks that stuck out of the floor. He was flat on his back and couldn't move.

"My pets haven't been fed this evening, and they're famished," said Ozzy. He pointed his umbrella at an enormous silo-sized feeder. "But why feed them seed, when tonight they can feast on a treat of meat?"

Ozzy grabbed a hanging control box and flipped a switch. All the cage doors clicked open. The birds screamed louder, pouring out of their cages.

Alfred's eyes widened in terror. He struggled against the ropes but couldn't budge.

Dozens of the loud, hungry birds darted toward Alfred. He turned his head away and shut his eyes in grim anticipation.

SMASH!

The worm-eaten wood of the vaulted ceiling burst inward. A large blurry shadow dropped into the center of the room, rolling with the fall and coming up right next to Alfred.

Ozzy's jaw dropped. "What's that?" he shrieked.

Alfred opened an eye — and saw a familiar mask looming above him.

13

Batman had no time to lose. He saw Alfred look up at him, but the birds were in a frenzy and diving fast. He crouched down beside his butler and threw his heavy cape over them both.

The birds attacked fiercely, slashing with their beaks and talons. Under the cape, Batman and Alfred waited for the birds to pause in their attack.

"What are *you* doing here?" asked Batman.

"Long story," said Alfred.

The birds ripped and pecked at the cape, and after a few moments, Batman heard it begin to tear. He stood up. He didn't want the rabid birds to fly through the torn areas and attack from underneath!

Batman swept his cape in a big circle, scattering the closest birds. In the same motion, he pulled a small metal disc from his Utility Belt and clicked a button on its side.

The disc was a sonic emitter. It was too high-pitched for human ears, but the birds hated the sound. They veered away from Batman, squawking as they scattered. They flapped toward the freshly made hole in the ceiling to escape the noise.

"No!" Ozzy shouted, horrified. "Come back, my pretties!"

The birds disappeared into the night, shedding gray and black feathers that fell like dark snow into the room.

"Jolly good," said Alfred, still tied down.

Ozzy glared at Batman. "So it seems the tales of the Batman are true." He sneered. "But really, who names himself after a mangy flying rodent?"

The masked women cartwheeled toward Batman from opposite sides of the room. This time, Batman was ready for them. With perfect timing, he jumped up out of the way, grabbing the bottom of a giant hanging cage. Below him, the masked women collided.

They stood and leaped upward, clinging to either side of the massive cage. But while they jumped, Batman somersaulted away, snapping open his Batarang and throwing it in one smooth motion before he landed.

The Batarang sliced through the chain holding the cage, sending it crashing to the ground — with the women. Before they could recover from the fall, Batman pushed them inside the cage. He snapped the Batarang around the door, locking them in.

"Your turn, Cobblepot," said Batman.

Ozzy smirked. He carefully took off his top hat and placed it on a table. "Please, now that all pretenses are off, call me Penguin — a flightless bird, but one with style . . ."

Then Penguin launched a sudden, powerful roundhouse kick that connected with Batman's head.

". . . and panache!" Penguin continued, with a spinning kick to Batman's stomach, knocking him down.

"My word," said Alfred, shocked at Penguin's unexpected gracefulness.

Penguin twirled his umbrella like a fighting stick. "Come on, rodent-boy."

Batman leaped to his feet and threw a punch, which Penguin easily blocked. *I really have to work on my speed training*, thought Batman. Penguin was surprisingly quick and hard to pin down.

Their battle took them all around the room, feet and fists and an umbrella whooshing through the air.

Alfred winced and rocked his body to either side to avoid being crushed underfoot in the battle. "Do watch your step," he implored.

Finally, Batman connected with a devastating combination of kicks and punches that sent Penguin reeling to the ground.

"Stay down, Cobblepot," ordered Batman.

The Penguin grinned and laughed in his quacking, honking way. "And have you miss this little treat?"

He stood and unraveled an evil-looking fighting chain from inside his umbrella. It was really long — almost a metal whip — and ended in a pair of razor-sharp steel talons.

Penguin whirled the chain overhead and whipped it toward Batman.

Batman twisted aside just in time. The talons sliced through a metal cage and sank into the floor beside Alfred's face. Alfred gasped . . . but then quickly realized that the whip had cut through one of his bonds. He began untying himself as quietly as he could.

Penguin yanked back the weapon and began whirling it again. "This Penguin's got claws!" he screeched.

Batman pulled two more Batarangs out of his Utility Belt, one for each hand. Again and again, the chain flew toward Batman, and again and again he blocked it with a Batarang.

Batman glanced down to check on Alfred. With a mighty effort, Penguin lashed the chain one more time and looped it around Batman's neck!

Before it could tighten around his throat, Batman dropped his Batarangs and stuck his hand between the chain and his neck.

Penguin pulled harder, trying to choke him. "Bird beats bat," he chuckled.

Batman strained to keep the chain off his

throat, then changed his tactic. He summoned up all his remaining strength and tugged on the chain as hard as he could.

Surprised, Penguin toppled forward toward Batman, who took advantage of the temporary slack in the loop to rear back his fist and land a huge punch.

Falling backward now, Penguin slammed into a giant silo of birdseed and crumpled into a heap beneath it. The impact shook out some loose birdseed onto his shoulders.

"There's a nice cage waiting for you, Penguin . . . in the Gotham state pen," said Batman, unwinding the chain. He turned and crossed the room toward Alfred.

Alfred stood up, finally untied. "As thrilling as it was watching you work, sir," he whispered once Batman had gotten close enough, "from here on out I shall leave the sleuthing to you." He grabbed his serving tray and prepared to exit.

On his way out, from across the room, Alfred noticed Penguin staggering to his feet and pulling out his sword.

"Behind you!" shouted Alfred. Before Batman could react, Alfred hurled his serving tray.

Penguin snorted as the tray missed him, soaring above his head.

The tray smacked into the big red lever attached to the huge silo, releasing an avalanche of birdseed.

"Ooph!" Penguin blurted as the birdseed smashed him to the ground and buried him.

Alfred dusted himself off, pleased. "That is for Grandfather Pennyworth!"

Sirens wailed in the distance. "We'll leave these birds for the police," said Batman.

"Birds?" asked Alfred, pointing at the large cage in which the two mysterious women had been locked. The cage was empty, except for their masks, which seemed to glow eerily in the candlelight.

"They flew the coop," said Batman. "I guess they squeezed through the bars."

He glanced back at Penguin, still unconscious beneath the birdseed. "He's not going anywhere, at least."

The sirens grew louder. "Time for us to fly, too, Alfred."

14

The sun beat down on the basketball court. Bruce Wayne and Ethan Bennett were nearing the end of a hard-played game of one-on-one. Bruce tried his best, but the fighting of the last few nights had taken its toll. Ethan spun around him to slam down the final point of the game.

"Wooo!" Ethan yelled, pumping his fist in victory. "That's game! Dogs are on you, dawg!"

Bruce nodded and smiled, trying to catch his breath. They walked to a snack cart, where Bruce bought them hot dogs and sodas. The two friends found a bench nearby to sit on.

As they talked and ate, Bruce tore off tiny pieces of his bun and tossed them to pigeons, thinking about the recent events. "Congrats on the Cobblepot bust, Ethan. Hard to believe such a big-time crook was at my party."

Ethan leaned toward him. "I can't take the credit for this one, Bruce. It's a big secret, but Gotham's favorite vigilante collared him for us." Ethan sat for a second in silence, then said, "You know, in some ways, I'm *glad* freaks like this Penguin bring out Batman."

Bruce sat quietly for a moment, too, his expression slightly troubled. "I just hope it's not Batman who brings out the freaks."

PART TWO

TRACTION

15

Gotham City was busy. It was always busy, even now, in the middle of the night, in an old, seemingly abandoned warehouse.

Two men stood in a pool of dim light coming from a bare bulb that hung down from the cracked ceiling. The men looked tough, but when they opened their mouths, their voices were shaky.

"Wh-why are we meeting *here*? Everyone knows he's attracted to shadows!"

The second man tried to seem calm, but his voice betrayed him. "R-relax, Batman th-thinks we split Gotham months ago."

"He dismantled my operation — brick by brick!"

"Yeah, well, he took down all my men, single-handedly. I can't even sleep at night!"

The two former crime bosses clutched their briefcases to their chests and waited.

A third man stepped from the shadows, also carrying a briefcase. His entrance startled the others. "Don't do that!" one hissed. "I thought you were Bat —"

"*Batman*, I know — he ruined me, too. But you can kiss those worries good-bye," said the third man, smiling evilly. "We've got the solution to our problem now."

"So what's the deal anyway?" asked the first man. "All you said was bring the money and we could get the Bat out of Gotham."

The third man raised his own briefcase. "It's for a mercenary — he volunteered for some physical enhancements in a secret lab, deep in the Amazon. Wild, huh? He says he'll do it, if we pay him."

The first two bosses nodded. "Well, we're in," said one, a little less scared than before. "Let's see him."

The third man whistled into the dark corner of the vast space. A figure appeared immediately, striding forward into the small area of light. He wore a skintight red-and-black outfit with yellow tubes running across it. His face was covered completely by a red-and-black mask. He seemed to be around the same size and build as Batman.

"Gentlemen," the third crime boss said dramatically, "meet Bane!"

The two other bosses looked at each other doubtfully.

"Uh . . . are you sure this guy can take down Batman?" asked the first boss.

"Yeah," piped up the second boss. "Just because he wears a mask doesn't mean he's some kinda *super*-man."

Bane chuckled deeply. One of the ports connecting the yellow tubes to his costume began to glow. "There is much more to me . . . than meets the eye."

16

Bruce had music blasting in the Batcave. The beats were thumping, the guitars were blazing. Bruce nodded to the rhythm, wearing large goggles and clenching a screwdriver in his teeth, as he tinkered with a collection of robotic devices spread out around him.

Alfred entered the Batcave, wincing at the loud music. He held a covered dish. "Master Bruce," he said.

No response.

Alfred rolled his eyes. "MASTER BRUCE!" he said again, much louder.

Bruce spun around, startled. He accidentally knocked over a robotic leg, which kicked out against Alfred's arm, sending the butler sprawling and overturning the tray of food.

Bruce smacked a button on a remote, shutting off the music. He rushed over to help Alfred back to his feet.

"Your nachos, sir," said Alfred, looking down at his jacket splattered with chips, beans, jalapeños, guacamole, and melted cheese.

Bruce spotted Alfred's torn sleeve and the scrape beneath. "Let me get that bandaged," he said.

Alfred shook his head. "It's merely a flesh wound. I do believe my military medical training has equipped me to handle such injuries." The butler glanced at the robotics distastefully. "And those would be for . . . ?"

"Don't know yet," said Bruce. "But they sure are cool. If only the engineers at Wayne Enterprises knew their cutting-edge technology was being used to assist Batman."

Alfred peered up at Bruce as he gathered the broken pieces of plate. "If only we could build a cleaning robot to assist Batman's *butler*."

Meanwhile, out on a dark, quiet street in Gotham, an armored car drove past on its usual route to the bank. The cargo compartment was loaded with stacked bundles of money. A guard sat beside the money, occasionally talking to the driver through a walkie-talkie.

Suddenly, the driver slammed on the brakes. Something was blocking the road.

BOOM! The back door of the armored car blew open, knocking the guard backward.

Bane appeared out of the smoke. He punched out the guard. Then he stood waiting as the driver radioed for help.

In the Batcave, Bruce was still working on the machinery. He twisted a screw on a large robotic arm and then pulled on a silver-and-black glove. He wiggled his fingers in the glove and the fingers on a robotic hand wiggled in response.

"Neat," said Bruce.

The computer screens began to beep and flash — a signal that the Bat-wave system had intercepted a call for the police. Bruce read the data streaming across the screen and narrowed his eyes.

Several seconds later, the Batmobile screeched away down a tunnel.

In the Batcave, the elevator door opened to reveal Alfred, holding another plate. "Nachos round two . . . Er, Master Bruce?" Then Alfred noticed the missing Batmobile, the tire marks leading away. He nodded and lifted the cover from the tray, sitting at one of the desks. He toasted the mess of robotics with a nacho.

"Cheers," he said, before crunching into the chip.

Detective Ellen Yin studied her police scanner computer intently. "We have an armored car assault — by an unknown masked assailant."

"Masked?" Her partner, Detective Ethan Bennett, raised his eyebrows.

"Maybe Batman decided being a vigilante didn't pay," she said wryly.

Bennett gestured toward the door. "After you," he said and they ran out of headquarters.

The Batmobile raced through the hidden tunnels that crisscrossed beneath Gotham. Batman checked a radar screen to make sure the coast was clear, then hit a button on the dashboard. A wall slid open and the Batmobile pulled out onto the street from an opening in the side of a freeway underpass. The wall slid shut behind him.

He sped down the road and stopped a few

blocks later, smoothly and almost silently, beside the armored car. Batman hopped out and strode over to the vehicle. He was shocked when he looked inside — the driver and the guard were tied up and gagged, lying on top of an incredible amount of bundled piles of cash. Nothing had been taken!

"I've been baited," murmured Batman. "Someone wanted to draw me out."

He spun around to see Bane standing behind him.

"Batman, I presume," said Bane.

Batman narrowed his eyes. "The 'mask look' must really be catching on," he said.

"Defeat me, and I will allow you to remove it," replied Bane.

Batman shook his head. "I don't fight for sport."

"Then fight for your life!" screamed Bane, charging at Batman. Bane threw a series of swift kicks and punches at Batman, which were all skillfully blocked. Batman had been practicing.

Now Batman fought back. Bane blocked his first attacks and leaped at him, snarling. Batman grabbed on and rolled backward, using Bane's momentum to flip the villain toward the side of the armored truck.

Bane slammed into the vehicle, denting it with the force of the impact. He slid to the ground as Batman stalked toward him.

"Talk to me," said Batman. "You can start with your name and motive."

"I am Bane," the masked villain replied through gritted teeth. "And I'm the last opponent you will ever face!" Bane's fingers reached for the glowing port above his wrist, sending fluid traveling through the yellow tubes that crossed over his back and chest.

Batman stared, dumbfounded, as he watched Bane's body begin to morph and stretch, bulking up to a monstrous version of his former self — several heads taller now than Batman!

Bane roared and swung a massive fist at Batman, who ducked under it. The giant hand smashed into a streetlamp, doubling it over.

Batman looked at the post and then back at Bane.

"Lights out, Batman," growled Bane, looming over him.

Batman pulled his Bat-grapnel out from behind

his back, where it was strapped to his Utility Belt. He fired it up at a three-story building and the tip sank into the very top, anchoring there. Gripping tight to the Bat-grapnel, Batman swung away and disappeared around the corner of the building.

Bane smiled hideously. "Go on," he yelled. "Flee from Bane!"

Batman emerged from the other side of the building, his momentum increasing all the way. Bane turned, surprised to see him, as Batman released the rope and slammed into him with both feet.

Batman landed and looked up in time to see Bane stagger only two tiny steps backward before straightening. Bane chuckled smugly.

Ducking under Bane's powerful swipes, Batman darted in close and landed a quick series of hard punches, but Bane didn't even seem to feel them.

Bane swatted down at Batman and missed, smashing the pavement. Batman jumped into the air and snapped open a Batarang, hurling it against Bane. It clattered to the street harmlessly.

Quickly, Batman pulled a capsule from his Utility Belt and threw it at Bane's feet. It exploded and smoke clouded around Bane for a moment. Batman waited, on his guard.

A huge set of arms emerged from the smoke. Bane was completely unharmed! Before Batman could react, Bane grabbed him and pulled him into an agonizing bear hug.

Batman gasped for air as Bane squeezed him tighter. He felt something crack in his chest. Bane lifted him up over his head and heaved Batman as hard as he could into a brick wall.

Slam! The wall crumbled with the impact, raining bricks down around Batman's twisted body. Bane turned back toward the tied-up men in the truck.

"Take the money! Take it!" mumbled one of them frantically through his gag.

Bane shrugged. "Pocket change." He grabbed the rear bumper with his meaty fists, heaved,

and flipped over the armored car onto its roof.

"With Batman gone, ALL of Gotham is mine!" Bane strolled away from the scene of destruction he had made — the overturned armored car, the dented lamppost, the shattered pavement, the collapsed brick wall. He disappeared into the night.

Under the pile of bricks, Batman lay still — his body battered, limp, and not moving.

18

A hand twitched. Then nothing.

The hand twitched again. An eye fluttered open. Batman let out a pained groan. His eye focused on the Batmobile parked nearby. He became aware of a faint sound: police sirens in the distance.

Batman tried to move, and groaned again with the effort. It hurt just to breathe. The Batmobile was so close, but not close enough. He gritted his jaw against the pain and tried again to start crawling. Some bricks shifted, but he couldn't move himself torward the Batmobile.

The sirens began to get louder. Batman's hand dropped to his Utility Belt, fumbling clumsily for the button to activate his com-link to the Batcave. "A-Alfred . . ." he gasped, ". . . need pickup . . ."

The sirens were even louder now, getting closer. Batman's hand slipped weakly from his belt, then he concentrated and grabbed for another button. A mini Bat-grapnel fired straight up into the air.

Behind the armored car, an unmarked sedan with a flashing siren screeched to a halt beside the Batmobile. Yin and Bennett leaped out, stunned by the sight of the Batmobile so close. "He's still here!" said Yin.

Bennett stared at the Batmobile in awe. "Check it out —"

Yin interrupted him, pointing at the wreckage. They carefully walked over to the open side of the truck, hands on their holsters. The detectives quickly spotted the guards and pulled their gags off. The guards were scared but basically unharmed.

"What happened?" asked Yin as she and Bennett untied them.

"Big guy," shuddered the driver. "Wears a mask . . ."

Yin nodded. "Batman?"

The guard shook his head. "*Bigger.* Threw Batman through that wall." He jerked his head toward the collapsed pile of bricks.

Yin and Bennett hurried over to the rubble that had covered Batman. He was gone.

The detectives looked at each other in surprise.

"Okay," said Bennett. "*If* a guy was buff enough to toss Bats through bricks . . ."

"There's no way Batman could have walked away from it," finished Yin.

Bennett nodded. "So where'd he go?"

19

Up in the dark sky of the Gotham night, three stories above Yin and Bennett, Batman hung limply in the air. He was dangling from the mini Bat-grapnel that connected his Utility Belt to the stone ledge of the roof.

Batman was in great pain, but he kept totally quiet so the detectives wouldn't hear him. A bead of sweat rolled down Batman's cheek and hung for a moment on his jaw before dropping off.

The two detectives had looked all around the collapsed wall, but couldn't find anything. They walked back to their car, the falling bead of sweat barely missing Yin.

Bennett reached in and grabbed the radio. "Dispatch, requesting all-points bulletin on masked suspect in the vicinity of Cherry and Montgomery. Be advised, perp is extremely dangerous."

Yin pulled the radio out of Bennett's hand, surprising him. "And send units to ALL area hospitals," she added. "We're looking for any new

admissions with multiple fractures." Yin clicked off. "If we find our patient, we find our Batman," she explained to Bennett. "Identity and all."

Suddenly, Yin got a strange look in her eye. Slowly, she turned her head up toward the sky, toward the building where Batman had been hanging. Too late. He was already gone.

Alfred trudged across the roof, Batman slung over his shoulder. He crossed to the other side of the building and then made his way slowly down the fire escape toward the ground. He was glad this was only a three-story building! Alfred's car waited for them in the alleyway below.

At the bottom, Alfred heaved Batman as gently as possible into the passenger seat of his gray Bentley. He pulled his mask off, and covered his body with a blanket, so no one would see Batman sitting in his car.

Alfred eased the car out toward the street, its motor purring quietly. When he reached the end of the alley, he was startled to see Yin and Bennett almost touching the Batmobile.

"What do you say we have a look inside?" Yin said.

"Yeah," said Bennett. He laughed. "Maybe the license and registration are in the glove compartment."

Inside his car, Alfred shifted uncomfortably. "Oh, dear," he said. He looked over at Bruce. "Uh . . . sir?" he asked.

Bruce's hand resting on his Utility Belt shifted slowly. Even though his eyes were almost closed, he was aware of what was happening around him — though just barely. With great effort, he felt around on his belt for the correct button and clicked it.

The Batmobile roared to life, shocking the detectives.

They leaped back as the Batmobile peeled out and rounded the corner at high speed, vanishing from sight. It cruised several blocks and slid into a secret tunnel hidden behind a wall. It would return to the Batcave on its own.

Alfred slipped away in the Bentley while the detectives were still distracted. Yin didn't spot them. As Alfred left the detectives behind, Yin was still staring angrily after the Batmobile, looking very frustrated.

20

Alfred drove through the Gotham streets, keeping one worried eye on Bruce slumped beside him. Bruce moaned faintly, the first sounds he had made in a while.

"We're nearly to the hospital, sir," said Alfred. "Shan't be a moment."

Bruce opened his eyes and stared at Alfred. He whispered painfully, *"Merely . . . flesh wound."*

Alfred felt puzzled. Then he realized what Bruce meant — he was quoting Alfred from a few hours ago! Was he really trying to say . . . ?

"I may have been a field medic many years ago," Alfred sputtered, "but I am hardly capable of — "

"Alfred . . ." whispered Bruce fiercely.

"You have broken bones, you may be bleeding internally — you need serious medical attention, Master Bruce!"

"No . . . hospitals," said Bruce, weakly but firmly.

Alfred shook his head, turning toward the

hospital. "I'm afraid it is out of your hands, sir. You see, we're already —" he began, but then he slammed on the brakes.

In front of him, three police cars were staked out at the entrance to the emergency room. Their lights were flashing. Alfred paused for a moment, and with a sigh of dread, turned the car around and headed for home.

Back at the warehouse, the three former crime bosses watched as Bane strolled toward them. He was back to his normal size.

The three men were grumbling. "I hear the cops are combing the hospitals, looking for Batman," said one.

"Yeah," said another. "I thought this guy was supposed to *end* our problems."

Bane calmly stepped forward. "If I did not break all of Batman's bones, I guarantee you, I broke his spirit."

The crime bosses exchanged a glance and then reluctantly handed their briefcases to Bane.

"Heh," laughed the third boss. "Don't spend it

all in one place."

Bane smiled darkly. "Oh, but I will . . . here in Gotham."

The crime bosses shifted uneasily.

"You see," Bane continued, "with Batman gone, there is no one to stop me!" He touched the glowing port on the back of his hand and began to grow. His muscles bulged as he looked down at the three men shrinking away from him. "Is there?" asked Bane.

The bosses fearfully shook their heads. Bane laughed and then stomped out of the building.

The first two men glared at the third, who had introduced them to Bane.

"So," said one angrily. "Who are you gonna find to get rid of him?"

"And with what money?" piped the second.

The third boss scowled back at them. "I hate masked men," he muttered.

21

Alfred's eyes shone worriedly above the surgical mask covering his nose and mouth. He snipped off the extra thread from a series of stitches and began to cast Bruce's leg with plaster.

Bruce lay peacefully, with an apparatus attached to his mouth to ease his breathing and his pain. Monitors were set up all around the operating table. Alfred wiped his forehead with a cloth, took a deep breath, and began casting one of Bruce's arms.

"Being summoned to pick you up has never been a good omen, Master Bruce."

Bruce's eyelids flickered. He heard Alfred's words as if from a distance. The words drifted through his mind, triggering an old memory . . . .

Bruce's big cheeks were dirty and streaked with the tracks of dried tears. He was just a child, a young boy. He sat in the police sergeant's office, the sergeant's cap too big on his head.

He kept looking down at the broken bracelet he gripped tightly in his hand. There were two pearls left on it. He almost began crying each time he looked at it.

Bruce forced his eyes away and stared blankly at the frosted glass in the door.

The door opened and the bareheaded police sergeant came in and smiled awkwardly at him.

"Lad," the sergeant said. "Someone's here for you."

Young Bruce looked up to see Alfred rushing toward him, looking absolutely heartbroken. Alfred was younger, too — it was about twenty years ago. "Master Bruce," said Alfred. He dropped to his knees to hug him.

"I am so very sorry," murmured Alfred. Bruce could see tears welling in Alfred's eyes and he clutched on to him, burying his head in the butler's shoulder. Alfred raised his chin and looked into Bruce's eyes. "I can never replace your parents, I know. But I promise you, I will never, ever leave your side."

Back in the Batcave, Bruce twitched slightly with the memory. Alfred noticed the movement and glanced at Bruce's face, seeing a half-smile there.

"That's it, Master Bruce," said Alfred through his surgical mask. "Be strong."

22

Yin and Bennett stared into a huge hole in the wall of a bank. Loose bricks, chunks of concrete, and twisted pieces of metal lay scattered around the gaping hole.

"Bane takes what he wants," said Detective Yin.

"And never cleans up after himself," added Detective Bennett.

A news van screeched up beside them. "Detectives!" shouted a reporter, shoving a microphone toward their faces. "Have there been any breakthroughs?"

Yin said calmly, "Rest assured — we're doing everything we can."

"What about Batman?" The reporter was talking very fast, trying to make his point before they stopped the interview. "It's rumored he hasn't been seen nor heard since this 'Bane' came on the scene."

Yin and Bennett exchanged a glance.

"We're operating under the assumption," said

Yin, "that Batman is no more."

The detectives walked away from the news van and got into their car.

The reporter turned to the camera. "There you have it," he said. "Gotham PD seems no closer to stopping this tremendous threat. It's been three weeks since the crime spree began, and the juggernaut known as 'Bane' still remains at large. Back to you, Jim."

In his room in Wayne Manor, Bruce clicked off the television. He was in bed, an elaborate system of ropes and pulleys rigged up to keep his legs and one of his arms elevated. The other arm was bandaged but movable, and he held the remote in that hand.

Alfred sat in a chair by his bedside, holding a protein shake that Bruce was sipping through a straw. "The police can't handle Bane," Bruce said when he finished drinking.

"Neither, apparently, could Batman," replied Alfred, earning a steely glare from Bruce. He rose and made a tiny adjustment to one of Bruce's pulleys, trying to make him more comfortable. "Do try and rest, sir," he said.

"Alfred," Bruce insisted. "Gotham needs Batman."

Alfred frowned. "Sir, I don't want to speak out of turn, but . . . if Gotham thinks Batman is no more, perhaps it is for the best." He put the protein shake on Bruce's bedside table. "Perhaps *Bruce Wayne* can heal and finally get on with his life."

Alfred left the room and went to prepare dinner. He returned an hour later to find Bruce's bed empty. He panicked for a moment, but then thought better of it and calmly went into the hall. He tapped a complicated pattern on the wall and one of the panels slid open, revealing a secret entrance into the Batcave.

He emerged from the elevator to see Bruce sitting in a wheelchair at one of the worktables. He held a tool in his bandaged hand and was clumsily working on the robotic equipment as best he could.

"And you are doing *what*?" asked Alfred.

"What you suggested," said Bruce. "Getting on with my life."

"Interesting interpretation, Master Bruce," Alfred said. "I just think you should know that if you intend to face this Bane again, you may need to find another butler/physician/getaway-car driver."

Bruce looked up sharply at Alfred. Could he mean it?

"I was barely able to save you this time, Master Bruce," explained Alfred gently. "I simply may not be capable of picking you up the next time you fall."

Bruce gazed at him, considering what Alfred was telling him. After a while, he said sincerely, "I understand, Alfred."

Bruce picked up his tool — a cross between a screwdriver and a pair of tweezers — and went back to working on the robotic leg. Alfred watched him sadly for a moment, then turned to leave.

A clattering sound made him turn back. He saw that Bruce had dropped his tool and was reaching determinedly for it.

It took a huge effort for Bruce to bend down, with his legs still stiff in their casts, his other arm sticking out gawkily. He couldn't reach the tool.

Bruce tried again, straining painfully, but again, it was just out of his reach. Alfred couldn't take any more. He picked up the tool, handed it to Bruce, and sat down beside him.

"Very well, then," sighed Alfred. "Let's get to work, shall we?"

A grin lit up Bruce's face.

23

Several nights later, Detective Yin was driving home after her night shift when the radio came on with a crackle.

"Attention, all units," the dispatcher's voice said. "Disturbance at 437 Adams, penthouse floor. There's a masked intruder on premises."

Yin knew that building. It was beautiful and luxurious and one block away from where she was driving. She grabbed her radio handset. "This is Yin. I'm in the neighborhood, I'll check it out."

Detective Bennett had just switched out the lights in his office. He had his coat half on and was almost out the door when he heard Yin's reply over the radio. He rushed back and picked up his handset.

"Yin, it's Bennett. I thought we were off duty?"

Yin responded coolly, "Guess Bane didn't get that memo."

"All right, I'm coming," said Bennett. "Wait

for my backup. Yin? Do you copy?"

Yin's handset lay unattended on her seat as she rushed into the lobby of the building. She ran past the doorman, flashing her badge, and rode the elevator up to the top. The elevator doors slid open and Yin stepped cautiously into the apartment.

She could see Bane across the room. He was bigger than ever and his tubes glowed in the darkness. He had torn a painting from the wall, revealing a huge safe that had been hidden behind it. Bane reached his massive arms around it and grabbed the sides of the safe, trying to pull it from the wall.

Cracks appeared around the safe. Yin drew her weapon nervously and took a deep breath, walking farther into the room. She aimed carefully before saying, "Gotham P.D.! Put your hands in the air!"

Bane whirled around, faster than could be imagined for someone his size, and plucked the weapon right out of her hand! Yin gasped as Bane crushed it in one burly hand, letting it drop to the ground in a twisted lump of metal.

He frowned at Yin, watching her grab a bronze

sculpture off the floor and throw it at him. Bane let it bounce off him and then swatted Yin across the room with a mighty backhand. She crashed into the far wall and sank to the floor, out cold.

Bane strode toward her, angry about being disturbed and ready to punish this police officer for being so rude. He raised his fist to beat down on her unconscious body, when he saw something from the corner of his eye. A movement.

He spun around as the elevator doors finished sliding open.

Batman walked out into the room, taller than Bane remembered. He looked strong in his new Bat-armor suit. The metal gleamed as Batman strode closer.

24

Inside the Bat-armor, Bruce was practically bandaged from head to toe. He had built the protective exoskeleton from robotic parts, and his arms and legs were held carefully inside the suit by more robotic devices. Instead of a mask, he wore a high-tech Bat-helmet that attached smoothly to the rest of the armor.

Despite the increased height of the Bat-armor, Bane still towered over Batman by at least a head. A faint beep in the helmet announced a Bat-wave transmission from Alfred. Bane would not be able to hear it — in fact, no sounds from inside the Bat-armor could be heard outside. Batman couldn't even speak through it!

"Master Bruce," crackled Alfred's voice. "How are things in the Bat-bot?"

"All systems go, Alfred," replied Batman. Seeing Bane rushing toward him, mighty fist cocked, he quickly added, "Over and out," and clicked off.

Batman threw a metal arm into the air and

blocked Bane's fist with a clank. He grabbed Bane and heaved him through a wall, out onto the roof deck. Bane staggered to his feet and leaped at Batman, nailing him with a heavy punch.

Batman backpedaled but the Bat-armor held strong and he did not topple over. He winced from the impact. They stormed over the huge roof deck, trading blows and blocks. The deck was very big, with potted trees, a hot tub, and even a helipad with a parked helicopter.

With both arms, Batman shoved Bane toward the helipad. Bane fell beside the helicopter as Batman clomped toward him. Bane reached one arm up and snapped the tail rotor right off the helicopter. He leaped up, snarling and slashing at Batman with the blade of the rotor.

Batman frowned at this development, then backed up slowly. Every time he blocked one of Bane's slashes, sparks flew outward from the impact of metal on metal.

Inside the apartment, Yin still lay unconscious. Detective Bennett burst into the room and rushed toward her.

"Yin!" He pulled out his walkie-talkie and clicked it on. "I need an ambulance: 437 Adams!"

He glanced around the room, taking in all the destruction. "And every available unit for backup!" he added.

A crash on the roof deck caught his attention and he stared through the smashed hole in the wall — seeing Bane and Batman battling fiercely outside.

Bennett paused for a moment before clicking the walkie-talkie back on. "Uh . . . dispatch — cancel the backup. Just the ambulance."

He pocketed his walkie-talkie and picked up Detective Yin, carrying her down to meet the ambulance.

25

Meanwhile, the battle continued to rage under the dark Gotham sky. From the roof deck, there was a beautiful view of the city, the tall stone and steel buildings stretching into the distance, lights twinkling in the night. Neither man took a moment to appreciate the view. They grunted with effort, fighting hard.

Bane swung the rotor once more and this time Batman caught it. With a sharp chop, he broke it into pieces. It fell from Bane's hand.

Batman swung three times, driving Bane down to his knees. As Bane dropped, Batman grabbed the giant's wrist and pulled at the glowing yellow port. It did not budge. He pounded at it, but Bane shook him off and growled, beating Batman back with three massive punches of his own, the strongest punches he had hit the Bat-armor with yet.

With each impact, Bane shouted, "You can NOT . . . BEAT . . . BANE!" The Bat-armor began denting from the force of the punches. Batman flipped backward and crashed to the deck, flat on his back like an overturned turtle.

Inside the Bat-armor, Bruce ached with pain. He looked up to see Bane looming over him.

Bane sank his fingers into the seams of the Bat-armor's chest plate and ripped it open like a tin can. Bruce's bandaged torso was suddenly open to the night air. The damaged armor sizzled and electricity sparked from torn cables that waved dangerously from the broken robotics.

Bane grabbed the jagged edges of the Bat-armor and pulled Batman toward him until they were masked-face to armored-face.

"I left you with some dignity last time. But now I will unmask you," hissed Bane. "And then I will shatter ALL the rest of your bones."

Bruce's mind was swirling, trying to come up with a plan. He had only seconds to spare.

Bane grabbed the Bat-helmet. No time left! Batman did the only thing he could think of — he grabbed one of the sparking cables and jammed it against the glowing port on the back of Bane's hand!

Bane's head snapped back and he screamed as electricity coursed through him, sparks flying everywhere. The port shattered like crystal, its glow instantly winking out.

He dropped Batman onto his back again as he began to suddenly grow even larger!

Bruce's eyes widened inside the suit. "Uh-oh," he mumbled.

Luckily, the growth spurt didn't last for long. The glow inside the tubes faded and Bane started shrinking, transforming back to his normal size. He collapsed to the roof, unconscious.

Bruce exhaled. He realized he'd been holding his breath for a long time. He and Bane lay beside each other, both flat on their backs. Bruce was awake, though, and Bane was out cold. Bruce smiled and clicked on the Bat-wave Transmitter.

"Uh . . . Alfred," he said. "I need a pickup."

He heard Alfred's sigh. "Of course, sir," the butler said dryly.

26

The television news report showed Bane, now merely the size of a normally large man, being led out of the hotel lobby in handcuffs by an entire squad of police officers.

"Bane was found unconscious at the scene, amid signs of a struggle," the reporter was saying. "But who Bane struggled *with* remains a mystery. Back to you, Jim."

Detective Yin clicked the remote and the television flickered off. She was lying in a hospital bed, wearing bandages and a cast on one arm. Bennett sat beside her, his feet up on her bed.

Yin shot Bennett a knowing look. "It was Batman, huh?"

Bennett pretended to be unsure. "Hard to tell. There was something different about him." He smiled and shrugged. "He saved your life, by the way."

There was a long pause.

"That doesn't change things, you know," she said finally.

Bennett gave a small sigh. "I know."

In the Batcave, one week later, the computer flashed and beeped. The Bat-wave symbol flashed an alert on the screen. Something was amiss on the streets of Gotham.

Bruce leaped up and pulled on his Batsuit. He stood on his own two booted feet. He swung his cape onto his back, pulled his mask over his head, and reached down for his gloves.

"Ow!" he said.

Alfred looked up sharply with concern. He was standing near the Bat-armor, which was almost finished being repaired.

"Will you be requiring the Bat-bot, sir?" he asked.

Batman pulled his gloves on and shook his head. "No, thanks, Alfred. I just need to watch those sudden moves." He winked and jumped off the circular platform on which they were standing.

"Jolly good, then, sir," said Alfred.

Batman hurtled down into the darkness, cape billowing out behind him.

Alfred heard the sound of the Bat-boat starting up below. "Jolly good," he repeated.